Disney
PRINCESS

THE PRINCESS AND THE FROG

LOOK AND FIND®

Written by Melanie Zanoza
Illustrated by Art Mawhinney

Published by Louis Weber, C.E.O., Publications International, Ltd.
7373 North Cicero Avenue, Lincolnwood, Illinois 60712

Ground Floor, 59 Gloucester Place, London W1U 8JJ

Customer Service: 1-800-595-8484 or customer_service@pilbooks.com

www.pilbooks.com

p i kids is a registered trademark of Publications International, Ltd.

Look and Find is a registered trademark of Publications International, Ltd.,
in the United States and in Canada.

8 7 6 5 4 3 2 1

Manufactured in China.

ISBN-10: 1-4127-1875-9
ISBN-13: 978-1-4127-1875-2

pi
kids ®   publications international, ltd.

Tiana wants to run her very own restaurant. But for now, she is working toward her dream by waitressing at Duke's Diner, one of her two jobs. As she heads into work, can you find these examples of New Orleans cuisine on Claiborne Street?

Pecan pie

KING CAKE

King cake

Beignets

PRALINES

Pralines

MUFFULETTA

Muffuletta

TODAY'S SPECIAL!!
JAMBALAYA

CRAWFISH

Crawfish

Jambalaya

The scheming Dr. Facilier has lured Prince Naveen and his valet, Lawrence, to his magic emporium. There, he is preparing to turn the prince into a frog! Look around the shop for these tools of the doctor's trade.

This bag of tricks

This magic potion

This Tarot card

This magic doll

This ceremonial drum

The talisman

This mask

At the LaBouffs' masquerade ball, Prince Naveen convinced Tiana her kiss would return him to his human form ... but now she's a frog, too! As Tiana and Naveen try to escape the mess they've created, help these famous couples find each other in the hubbub.

Antony and Cleopatra

Romeo and Juliet

Lancelot and Guinevere

Robin Hood and Maid Marian

George and Martha Washington

Adam and Eve

Tiana and Naveen escaped to the bayou, where they found some friends, Louis and Ray. As the two new frogs adjust to their surroundings, look around the swamp for these Cajun creatures they've yet to meet.

Teal

Water moccasin

Catfish

Butterfly

Kingbird

Heron

Dragonfly

Tiana and her friends have arrived at the home of Mama Odie, the blind 197-year-old good magic lady. While she determines what the frogs need, look around the galley of her old shrimp boat for these things Mama Odie needs.

Juju

Jar of candy

This jar of powder

Hot sauce

This magic potion

Gourd

Naveen has escaped from Dr. Facilier's trap just in time. While he chases after the magic talisman, look around the festivities for these oblivious revelers enjoying the parade.

This flambeaux thrower

This genie

This can-can dancer

This mermaid

This Greek god

This pirate

Tiana and Naveen are human again ... and married! As they prepare to celebrate their happily ever after, look around for these delighted guests.

Louis

Mama Odie

Eudora

Charlotte

Queen

Big Daddy

King

All of Tiana's dreams seem to be coming true! First she found her prince, and now she's opened her restaurant. Look around the busy dining room for these items every great restaurant should have.

Menu

Opening-day photo

Grand Opening

Banner

Reservation book

Lucky horseshoe

Newspaper review

Catch the streetcar back to Claiborne Street and say hello to these people Tiana passed on her way to Duke's Diner.

Sneak back to Dr. Facilier's magic shop and look for 40 black candles.

Twirl back to the LaBouffs' backyard and look for these revelers.

Ray's firefly family is a big help to Tiana and Naveen. Do you see some of them in the bayou?

Mama Odie loves her gumbo! Scout around her boat for these ingredients she'll need for her next batch.

The parade-float riders threw all sorts of trinkets to the happy crowd. Do you see these necklaces of colorful beads around the square?

Jackson Square is always filled with artists. Can you find these paintings amidst the wedding celebration?

Tiana worked very hard to make her dreams come true. Do you see these hard workers at her restaurant?

Sea Star Wishes

Poems from the Coast

With best wishes!

ERIC ODE

Illustrated by ERIK BROOKS

SASQUATCH BOOKS
SEATTLE

To my daughter, Lauren, who finds great joy in tide pools,
mud flats, and singing in the rain. With love, Dad. —E.O.

Manufactured in China by C&C Offset Printing Co. Ltd. Shenzhen,
Guangdong Province, in December 2012

Published by Sasquatch Books
17 16 15 14 13   9 8 7 6 5 4 3 2 1

Editor: Christy Cox
Project editor: Nancy W. Cortelyou
Illustrations: Erik Brooks
Design: Anna Goldstein

Library of Congress Cataloging-in-Publication Data is available.

ISBN-13: 978-1-57061-790-4

Sasquatch Books
1904 Third Avenue, Suite 710
Seattle, WA 98101
(206) 467-4300
www.sasquatchbooks.com
custserv@sasquatchbooks.com

LOOK

Gulls soar.
Grasses bend.
Waves roar;
they rise
and fall
and thunder.
And all say,
look,
watch,
wonder.

THE SEA URCHIN

Let's search
for the sea urchin
here in the salty spray,
where sunlight shines
on his stay-away spines,
flashing red and purple
in a storm of gray.

Let's search
for the sea urchin,
you and me.
We'll find him alone,
clinging to a tide pool stone,
that thistly,
bristly
hedgehog of the sea.

THE BARNACLE

Startled,
the barnacle
hunkers to hide
until she is only
a stony, cone-shaped shell,
silent and still,
in the shallow tide.

But when I stop
and when I sit
and when I watch
and wait a bit,
she reappears to dance about,
in and out,
this way and that,
like a feather on a fancy hat
caught in the wind.

THE FERRY BOAT

Back
      and forth
and back
      and then,

  back
      and forth
and back
      again.

That steely beast,
like Jonah's whale,
takes his fill,
groans and rumbles,
lumbers slowly
west to east
across the sound.

But that oh-so-clever creature
never stops
to turn around,
never circles back.
Instead,
what was his tail
becomes his head.

THE LIGHTHOUSE

Lighthouse.
Bright house.

Sturdy red-and-white house.
You know what waits
beneath the tide.

You know where rocks
and dangers hide.

Find the ships.
and steer them wide.

Lighthouse.
Bright house.

Watchman-of-the-night house.

THE STUNT KITE

The stunt kite
        does not
            fly.
It swoops
        and loops.
  It circles
        and lunges,
     lurches,
       dives,
        climbs,
         and plunges.

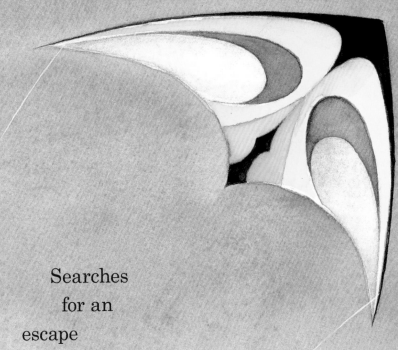

Searches
for an
escape
from the anchor
of the beach.
Pulling as if
it were trying to
scribble
on the sky
but can't
quite
reach.

SEA STAR WISHES

Do sea stars make wishes
on stars of the night
and dream that they might
be as shiny and bright?

And if they make wishes,
perhaps it could be
that fishes make wishes
on stars of the sea.

THE LIMPET

How simple
the life
of the limpet,
sitting alone
in her dome of a home,
tucked out of sight
with little to do
but sleep
and dream
and hold
on
tight.

WRINKLES

On the narrow pier,
grandfathers
lean
against the gray railing
and use their
fishing line
to play a lazy game
of tug-of-war
with the water.

While here
on the shore,
the waves
ripple
against the sand

like a quiet grandmother
trying to smooth
the last wrinkle

from a stubborn
bedsheet.

THE GEODUCK

Who's that stuck
among the muck
beneath the ocean floor?
Whose neck is that?
It's strong and fat
and three feet long or more.
    Who has no nose?
    Who has no ears?
    Who lives one-hundred-fifty years?
Who gives a squirt,
then disappears
into the sand,
into the muck?
    Who can it be?
    The geoduck!

The name geoduck means to dig deep, and
you pronounce it like this: GOO•ee•duck.

THE EEL

It's true he looks appalling,
but still I have a feeling
another eel
(a mother eel?)
might find the eel appealing.

THE HERMIT CRAB

The hermit crab,
the hermit crab.
He never takes
a taxi cab;

or sails a ship
or submarine;
or rides a motorbike
  machine.

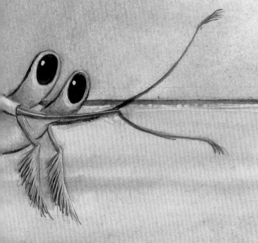

He never skips
across the sands
but skitters on
his pointy hands.
And with his home
upon his back,

he never worries
what to pack
or what to drive
or what to wear
to get from here
to over

there.

THE OCTOPUS

How odd to think the octopus
has not a bone inside her.
The smallest space in any place
is just enough to hide her.
A corner in a sunken ship,
a coffee can,
a shell.
She tucks her boneless body in
and every arm as well.
A very tricky thing to do
if you have one
or maybe two.
But what an awkward sort of state,
the octopus has eight!

THE DECORATOR CRAB

Sing a song
to celebrate
the decorator crab.
She adores a finely furnished home,
deplores those places
plain and drab.
And so she gathers
bit by bit
those things that bring her pleasure,
selecting cherished pieces
like some secret
stolen
treasure.

A scrap of sponge
to set in place.
A frond of kelp
like leafy lace.
A tentacled anemone.

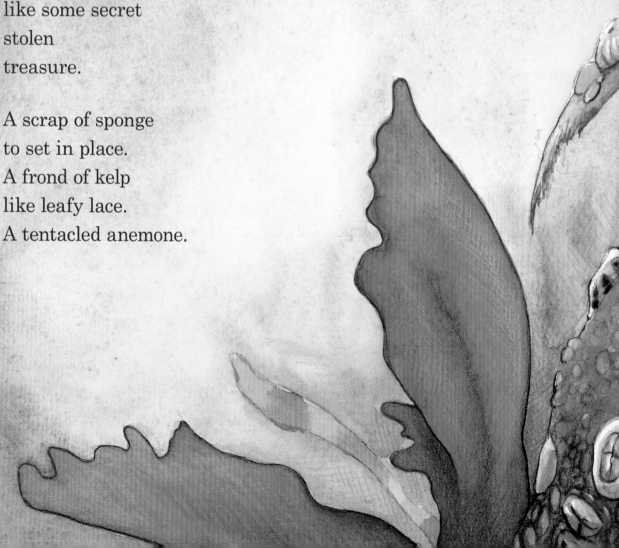

She places each
where it should be.
But as she has no walls or halls,
no windowsill or shelf,
the ever-clever decorator
decorates herself.

THE JELLYFISH

The jellyfish is not a fish
and doesn't look the part.
He has no snout to nose about.
He has no brain or heart.
He has no gills. He has no fins.
(He has a mouth but never grins.)
He has no eyes. He has no scales.
He has no splishy, fishy tails.
It seems, in fact, he's mostly belly
dressed in tentacles and jelly.

THE SEA LION

When you are
the lion of the sea,
even the sturdy wooden dock
floating stubbornly on the water
must bow down
to the massive weight
of your majesty.

THE SEA CUCUMBER

Here comes the sea cucumber
in his slumberly, lumbering way,
with little tube feet too many to number,
and little or nothing to say.

He's not one to cuddle or snuggle in tight.
He's not one to hug or to tickle.
But still he may wish you to kiss him goodnight,
and, my, wouldn't that be a pickle!

THE SANDCASTLE

Somewhere in this sandcastle,
upon a sandy chair,
there sits a tiny, sandy queen
who combs her sandy hair.

And somewhere there's a sandy king
with sandy velvet collars.
He's eating sandy sandwiches
and counting his sand dollars.

And somewhere there's a sandy prince,
handsome, brave, and tall.
He dreams he'll meet his sweetheart
at the royal sandy ball,

with softly soaring music
and the flickering of candles,
and fine glass slippers on her feet.
Or maybe she'll wear sandals.

STORIES

Who wrote these stories
here on the shore;
the strange little riddles
of who came before?

Some stamped and some stippled,
some scribbled, some scrawled,
where someone has waddled
or slithered or crawled.

A gull and a heron,
a crab and a loon.
A young, muddy puppy,
a crafty raccoon.

Some weave and some wander.
Some march in a line.
And others, like those
with their ten naked toes,
are mine.

THE MOON SNAIL

"How soon?" says the moon snail
   from under the sand.
"How soon till the gull
   and the loon understand?
The sun's on the water
   and waits for a tune."
"How soon?" says the moon snail.
"How soon?"

"Not long," says the plover
   from over the sea.
"The gull and the loon
   and the water agree.
They'll fly to the sun,
   and they'll bring her a song."
"Not long," says the plover.
"Not long."